Jack the Feral Prince
A Rags to Riches Story

Marianne & Sofia – all the best – Jack + Suzie

ISBN 1-4196-2067-3

Library of Congress Control Number: 2005910713

To order additional copies, please contact us.
BookSurge, LLC
www.booksurge.com
1-866-308-6235
orders@booksurge.com

This book is dedicated to all those who gave of their time, talent, energy, and support to this project. My thanks and deepest gratitude to you - my family and friends...

SD

Note from the editor ~

"What is a feral cat? Feral cats are the wild offspring of domestic cats and are primarily the result of people failing to spay or neuter their cat. These cats stay alive as best they can - near restaurants, shopping centers, parks, dumps, or in rural areas. Feral cats often live in loose groups, or colonies, and usually go out of their way to avoid human contact. No one knows the exact feral cat population of the United States, but it is estimated that there are millions. Without human intervention, many of these cats have short, painful lives. Many organizations and individuals have made heroic efforts to help these animals." ~K.W.

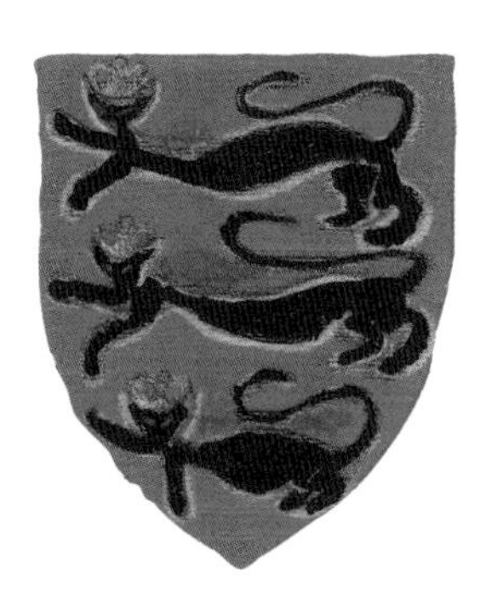

CHAPTER ONE

My earliest memories were of safety, warmth and happiness - I remember cuddling up with my brother and sister while under the watchful gaze of my Mom. We woke up to nurse, groom and play, and received endless, loving nuzzles from her - life was purr-fect.

Our home was in a barn, and Mom kept us close to her under the shelves. She warned us on a daily basis to stay under the shelves and out of sight from the people when she was away hunting. That was easy to do when we were tiny, because we slept so much that it seemed as though she was always there. However, as we started to get bigger, we grew curious about what else might be in the barn. Sometimes when Mom was out hunting, we would sneak out from under the shelves and go on exploring adventures. There were all different types and sizes of boxes to climb and jump up on, stuff to sniff, and plastic pipes that we would crawl into from one end and play chase out the other. The hay in the barn was a lot of fun too! But, we were always sure to quickly sneak back under the shelves before Mom came back and caught us.

Mom would bring us mice, gophers and an occasional rat. She told us that as we got older, she would take us out and teach us how to hunt for them ourselves. There seemed to be plenty of things for us to do in the barn, and mom kept our tummies full. Once we finished eating, she would give us each a loving cleaning and then we would curl up for a good nap.

I very vividly remember one particular morning, I awoke suddenly to an awfully loud noise - the eyes of my siblings were wide open too. I quickly glanced around, but Mom was nowhere in sight. We heard the people making a big ruckus and we were worried for not only our safety, but for Mom's too. The people had made loud noises before, but she was always with us to keep us calm and safe. Where could she be? I didn't feel very safe right now! Boxes were being over-turned and hay bales were being lifted and then dropped - the people seemed to be looking for something. In the corner of the barn they turned over a big box and finally found what they were looking for - Mom! One of the people snatched her up by the neck in a mean and nasty way - Mom fought with all of her might. She was scratching and hissing and clawing at the people. That was something she taught us to do if we were ever grabbed and needed to get away - only Mom wasn't getting away. The people were yelling at her now and shaking her hard. After a time, Mom stopped fighting - I wasn't quite sure why. Finally they put Mom back in the box and left the barn. My siblings and I didn't know what to do. We waited a long time and Mom never returned to us under the shelves. It didn't even look like she was trying to get out of the box. After a while longer, when it started to get dark and we were all feeling hungry, I decided to go check on her. My brother and sister stayed under the shelves and I told them I would be right back. There were no other sounds in the barn and the people were no where in sight.

I carefully crawled out from under the shelves and crept slowly across the barn floor to the box where Mom was. When

I looked inside, it seemed as if Mom was asleep. I sniffed her, and licked her but she didn't move. I called softly to her but she didn't stir. Scared and confused, I headed back under the shelves, and the three of us curled up, very hungry and missing Mom.

In the morning, I woke up and looked around for Mom, but then remembered the day before. I peered out from under the shelves only to see that the box and Mom were still there. My brother and sister were awake and looking to me for answers - what were we supposed to do, I wondered.

About that time, there was a flurry of noise coming from outside of the barn. The people were coming again, but this time, the voices were ones that we hadn't heard before. I was sure because, when they entered the door, their voices were very soft and gentle sounding. They walked over to the box where Mom was lying and they talked for a while. They began to look around for something else and I wondered why I wasn't scared. I think it was the soothing sounds that their voices made - not at all like the other people. They looked in all the nooks and small places in the barn until they came upon the shelves. They were looking for us! One of them reached in, grabbing me by the scruff of my neck - I kicked, hissed and scratched just as mom had taught me. Unfortunately, I was no match for the people. The gloves they were wearing protected them from our sharp, little claws and teeth. There were two of them, and once they grabbed all three of us they placed us carefully into a cage. We huddled together in the corner, cold and very scared. The people talked soft and gentle to us.

Mom had told us in the past about cars and trucks and it looked as though we were headed toward one of them. Once we were loaded in, the people talked to us, but it was hard to understand everything that they said. They used the words "safe" and "food" which helped us start to feel a little more comfortable, and also spoke fondly of a place called the "rescue barn".

Once we arrived, we were taken into a large structure - even bigger than our barn. There were tons of other kittens and cats in cages much like ours. Each one of them had a different story to tell about how they came to this place. We were told that this is where cats, which are rescued, wait for a new and safe home - this must be what "rescue barn" means. We were considered "feral" cats they said. We figured that must mean we did not have a family or a home, or something wild like that. The people put a blanket in our cage, along with food, water, and a litter box (another thing we had only heard of). We quickly gobbled up all of the food, and drifted off to sleep, sensing that we were a little safer now.

Every day it seemed as though several cats left and more arrived. We stayed in our cage, and although we were scared of the people, we felt safe with each other. Some number of days after we arrived, each of us was seen by the doctor - we were given shots, marked, and neutered. By the time we were ready to learn how to hunt for ourselves we were in a car again for a ride to our new home. We had been adopted!

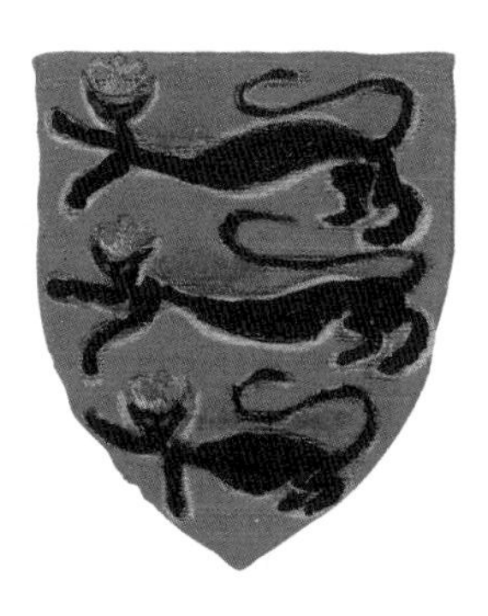

CHAPTER TWO

Once the car stopped, we were transported in our cage to a barn. It smelled just like the barn we had lived in with Mom and that made me think about her. At the same time I felt uneasy, as memories of the mean people flashed in my mind. There were new people in this barn, however, and they sounded happy and excited to see us. My brother, sister and I stayed huddled up together in the corner of the cage - we were quite leery about what might happen to us next. They placed our cage carefully in a corner of the barn, when all at once, we caught the scent of something completely new - it was a dog! He must have been about ten times our size. With his thick brown fur and big muscles, he approached our cage - thank goodness it was closed. His slobbery nose sniffed and sniffed all around the outside of the cage. The new people called the dog and he was soon out of sight. They rested two bowls inside the cage, which held fresh water and food for us. As soon as the people left the barn and it was quiet, the three of us quickly ate and drank and then fell fast asleep huddled in our blanket - what a day it had been!

The next morning was very tranquil. I could see outside

through a broken slat in the barn's door. The sun rose slowly over the magnificent green hills, scattered with colorful wild flowers. Soon the new people arrived and checked on us - they seemed gentle and nice. During the day the barn door was left open, and from time to time we would get a visitor - the dog. He would often lay down right next to our cage and take a nap. He seemed very curious about us and asked many questions. But I just kept quiet, as I didn't know if we could trust him. He did tell us that he had never met cats before. When he was asleep, I would sniff him through the cage. He had a myriad of smells on him! I could smell the new people, his food, the hay and unusual smells that were new and interesting to me - smells like dirt and plants that I was eager to explore. We were all starting to wonder what it would be like outside of the cage. My brother, sister and I were beginning to feel a little more at home.

As the days went by the new people made sure that our cage was clean, that we had plenty of food and water, and they talked softly to us, being careful not to startle us or try to touch us. My brother and sister were counting on me to take care of them. They would huddle behind me in our little blanket while I hissed and scratched at the new people so they wouldn't try to pick us up. What a show I put on - I felt just as frightened they did! We had seen what the mean people did to our mom, and we weren't keen on trusting these people, nice or not.

Day after day, that darn dog just sat there with his drippy nose, sniffing, sniffing, SNIFFING! When I sniffed back, he would get so over-excited that he made a fool of himself barking and jumping at the cage, urging us to come out. Of course, all that did was scare us so badly that we retreated to our blanket in the corner.

Almost a month passed when one morning the people came into the barn and made a big change. When they filled up our food and water bowls, they set them outside of the cage, making sure to leave the cage door ajar. On their way out, they closed the barn door so no one could come in or go out. Very interesting!

At first we just crouched together in the bed, but curiosity and hunger soon took over. I volunteered to go first. I carefully crept to the cage door and stepped out on the soft floor. Surprisingly, nothing happened. So I took a few more steps toward the food bowl and began to eat my breakfast. My brother and sister just watched me in amazement. Once my belly was full, I managed to coax my brother to the cage door. He stepped out, took a few bites and then quickly scurried back into the cage. My sister decided that it just wasn't worth the risk.

Now that I had been out of the cage and the barn door was secure, it seemed like a good time to explore in the barn. The barn must have been fairly old, as its slats had become splintered and rickety. It was obvious from the scents all around that there were many kinds of animals that had lived here - horses, cows, dogs, and other cats. I even smelled mice and small rodents like the ones that Mom used to catch and bring us for supper. I wondered if someday I could catch a mouse on my own since Mom hadn't had the opportunity to teach me. My brother came out of the cage now, and we explored together most of the morning. We found that there were more comfortable places to sleep than that old cage. It took almost half the day before our sister came out - she was eager mainly to find good hiding places. We showed her that there was a place under the floorboards that would be perfect, plus it was warm and dry. By the end of the day, we were familiar with every nook and cranny in the barn. We wore ourselves out so much that we slept through the entire night as if we had nothing left to fear.

The next morning we woke up to the sounds of the people coming into the barn. They were happy to see that we had been brave enough to venture out of the cage. Quietly, they refilled our food and water bowls. They whispered to us like we were part of their family and off they went leaving the barn door wide open. The three of us took turns nibbling on breakfast when all of a sudden ... guess who came in to see us - the dog! He immediately headed toward our cage. He sniffed and sniffed, finally realizing that we weren't in there - probably not the smartest dog in the neighborhood. Then he proceeded to eat the remainder of our food - what nerve! While he was chowing down, he seemed to get a scent that caught his attention. He set out straight toward our safe place under the floorboards. All we could do was lay there shivering in fear. We didn't know if he wanted to eat us or play with us. I soon figured out that he must have felt that this was the perfect opportunity to get to know us, but we surely didn't feel that way about him. He was just so big and rough and clumsy. My brother and sister cowered behind me - it seemed as though it was up to me to show him what was what. As he bounded toward us, I hissed and growled, but he didn't get the hint at all. Once he got close enough, I took a good swipe at his nose with my sharp claws - ouch! He abruptly jumped backward and let out a yelp - his feelings and his slobbery nose were both hurt. Now he didn't want to play at all - it was clear by the look on his ugly mug, he intended on showing me how superior he was. This time when he lunged toward me, I charged right back and took another swipe at him - ouch again! He let out another yelp and swiftly backed away and scampered out the barn door. We were very lucky but definitely still scared and hungry.

CHAPTER THREE

The next morning we were fed at the normal time, and once again, the barn door remained open. After eating, the three of us discussed the option of venturing outside and weighed our odds. We decided that my brother and I would check out our surroundings and my sister would stay behind in the barn - the last thing we wanted was for other animals to smell the scent of her fear. With the whole day ahead of us, we were so excited to check out the world outside the barn. I was headed out the door, with my brother close behind.

The first thing I noticed was the immense open space. It was peaceful and filled with delightful aromas - hopefully the dog was somewhere else. I was careful to make sure that any direction we headed, there was a place to scurry into, in order to quickly elude the dog or the people. It was springtime, so the wild flowers were abloom and the trees held buds in all shades of green. Instinctively, my brother and I were drawn to a tree with the most jagged bark. We scratched and scratched, sharpening our claws until our paws were tired. It wasn't long before the world around us started waking up, so we headed back to the barn - we would most probably have many more days of exploring ahead of us.

Once we returned, the first thing I did was head to the floorboards for a long nap. We must have been really worn out because we slept until mid-afternoon. When I awoke, I stretched and climbed up into the barn. Apparently the people had returned to check on us sometime while we were out. My sister said that they had refilled our food bowls - they must have figured out that the dog had some seriously bad manners. It was as good a time as any for a snack ... so I settled in to nibble the kibble. It wasn't long before I noticed that I was being watched - it was another dog! Yep, there stood a second one right in the doorway. Luckily, this one seemed a bit more reserved. His fur was dark brown, black and white, with a long fluffy tail and he appeared to be a bit shorter than our brown dog. I slinked away from the bowl in hopes of making a quick escape back to the floorboards. To my surprise, he very calmly walked in and carefully sniffed around the barn to pick up our scents. Then he looked directly at me and stated that his name was Buddy and that he lived next door with some really nice people. He went on to say that his people had a cat and he understood that the cat was the boss. How nice - maybe he could teach the other dog some manners. He asked me if he could take a nap in our barn, as the walk back to his yard was lengthy. I looked at my brother and sister, who were both peering out from under the floorboards and let the dog know that it was alright and that we would also share a little of our food with him. At first I didn't understand why I was quick to agree - I later realized, after talking with my siblings, that he made us feel safe and might protect us from our unfamiliar surroundings.

As each day came and went, a routine developed between the people and the three of us. The people always talked softly and urged us to come out and get our food the instant the bowls were filled. They frequently scolded the dog and asked him to mind his manners where we were concerned. What's more, they enlightened him by explaining that we were his kitties. Imagine that, we were the responsibility of the dog. There wasn't a time that these new people had ever raised their voices or threatened us in any way. They were slowly but surely becoming our people, and we were becoming their cats.

It became evident that one person in particular had taken on the daily chore of refilling our food and water. Each morning, as she spoke softly to us, she would make sure that she caught a glimpse of each of our faces under the floorboards. I decided that a test was in order, so I came out to take a closer look while she filled our bowls. She acted as if she didn't realize I was right behind her, but I was certain that she saw me. It was like we were playing a game with each other. After a couple of weeks, I couldn't stand it any more, so I mustered up all the nerve that I could, and took a huge risk - I rubbed up against her leg. She continued to talk softly to me, and fill the bowls - she didn't even try to touch me. Later on that day, she returned with another one of the people. He patiently stood and waited until I rubbed up against both of them. He very gradually leaned down and offered me something that Mom had told us about - CHEESE! It was extraordinary! I was so lost in delight that I didn't realize he was stroking my back. I purred and drooled all over - absolute heaven! Once they were gone, my siblings berated me, suggesting that I had lost my mind. The memories of what had happened to our mom were still fresh in their minds, but they would soon realize what they were missing out on...people to love us.

CHAPTER FOUR

Being a feral cat was all that my siblings and I understood, until our people showed us that being part of their family was significantly more satisfying. We had a safe home full of entertainment, adventures and lots of love. We were also given names - my brother, Alex, my sister, Morris, and me, Black Jack - everyone just called me Jack.

Alex, the biggest of the three of us, sports a torn ear and vivid black and white markings. Morris' multi-colored fur makes her look like she's wearing a funny black and brown coat with a white tipped tail. Of course the most handsome cat in the family is me, all black and exceptionally athletic. We each have a small hole at the top of the right ear - the people at the rescue barn put it there as a mark so that the doctor only gave us our shots and neutering once.

Our people made it clear that they depended on us to eat small rodents and lizards that attracted rattlesnakes around the property. It was easy to determine the perimeter, as a nice new fence had been built. They continued to leave a bowl of food out for us each day along with fresh water, to make sure we had a balanced diet, yet we knew instinctively that we had a job to do. I worried about whether or not I would succeed in becoming a good hunter since my mom hadn't taught us how to hunt before we lost her. I hoped that the stories that mom had shared with us when we were young, and sparring with each other as kittens, would give us a head start.

I will never forget one particular day. It was very early in the morning and I happened to be the only one awake. The sound of hard rain on the barn's roof woke me, so I took the opportunity to laze around a little while my siblings slept. I was just delving into a leisurely bath in the soft hay when I heard a rapid scratching sound - it seemed to be coming from the back of the barn. I stayed motionless on my back while trying to determine what it could be. Out of the corner of my eye, I spied a tiny field mouse - I remained frozen in position. The mouse was so intent on our food bowl that he didn't even notice me. This was my chance! I did what I thought a good hunter would do - I lunged toward the mouse with my claws fully extended and snatched him up by the scruff of his neck - he didn't move after that. I wasn't quite sure what to do with it. I carried it around, boasting to Alex and Morris and then went outside the barn to show our people. They praised me with joyful words and told me to drop the mouse so that they could scratch my ears. Unfortunately, as soon as I did, the mouse took off! Apparently, playing dead wasn't just a cat trick. It quickly became a game of cat and mouse, and the good guys won! Morris and Alex had a taste of my prize, and I wasn't hungry for the remainder of the day - let's just leave it at that. I could tell that Morris would know how to catch one, but Alex seemed perplexed. That's the thing about Alex, he has always had that confused look on his face - maybe it was just stuck there. After a nap, we discussed the hunt. I could tell that he was still puzzled about whether to freeze first, or pounce first, so I took Alex outside the barn to practice. Morris just rolled her eyes and went to the corner for a bath.

We hadn't wandered far before we came upon a bird feeder near the house flurried with little yellow finches. Although I didn't think finches would make a good meal, there were plenty of them to practice our technique on. We sat in the shade while I specifically explained to Alex each detailed step that he would need to take. We spent quite some time watching before Alex thought he might be able to give it a try, but he wanted me to go first. It wasn't long before a few of the finches fluttered to the ground to gather fallen seeds. Camouflaging myself in the shadows, I slowly slinked close to the ground, creeping closer and closer. Alex watched intently as the finches went about their business. Once I had strategically chosen one that was closest to me, I lunged and scored! I had him in my mouth before Alex could blink. I thought that Alex had grasped the concept, so I let the bird go - now it was his turn.

Alex stood up and walked over, causing all of the birds to flutter away. I told him that if he stayed right there and was patient, they might come back. He plopped down to wait as I returned to the brush to supervise. It seemed like forever, but sure enough, the finches returned one by one. I wondered why Alex wasn't pouncing at them - he had plenty of opportunities. It didn't take long for me to come to the conclusion that Alex had fallen asleep! When one of the finches landed close to him, he was so startled that he jumped, and all of the birds flew away! I calmed him down and told him that I would sit next to him and talk him through the process in case they came back. To this day, if it weren't for the food bowl in the barn, Alex would starve. Regardless of the outcome, there we were, just the two of us, making what I knew would be great memories.

My sister, Morris

My brother, Alex

CHAPTER FIVE

While exploring the area around our home, I encountered many rescued feral cats who had found homes around the neighborhood, as well as several domestic cats that briefly meandered outside of their houses for a little sunshine and fresh air.

It was apparent that each of us had a routine, as well as a territory based on the amount of food available within the proximity of our homes. This was also true within our family. Morris' special area was close to the outside of the barn where one of our people spent time doing chores and projects. She had the benefit of having her ears scratched and her tummy rubbed, which she loved. She also kept the inside of the barn clear of rodents and lizards. She taught me how to catch a snake, although I wouldn't recommend it to any cat, especially after being warned by other ferals about rattlers. I learned exactly what they were talking about one hot summer day. There was a small bush close to the people's house, which moved ever so slightly and made a funny buzzing noise. Of course, I went over to investigate - the closer I got, the more rapid the rattle became. At first I thought it might make a fun new toy, so I jumped on top of the bush. To my surprise, it wasn't the bush making all of that noise - there seemed to be an underlying factor. Whatever it was, the more I jumped at it, the more frenzied it seemed to get. Luckily, Alex appeared behind me and instinctively hissed and growled a warning to me. Not only did this prompt me to back off, but it alerted our people, who immediately came to our rescue. Looking back, I realize how lucky I am to have such a great brother, and to have our people, who taught us a very crucial lesson that day.

Alex hung out around the deck of the house and kept an eye out for wild animals such as skunks and raccoons, which tended to scavenge our food bowl and dirty up our water. He also made the decision as to which stray cats we would share our food with. In fact, that was Alex's finest trait - the welcome wagon - good thing since he was such a terrible hunter. It took a lot of cheese and patience for Alex to allow our people to scratch his ears, and while he enjoyed the love and attention, he considered his job of watching out for our space to be of the utmost importance. He quickly learned that his muscular stature and intimidating growl did not terrify any of the other animals, instead it endlessly annoyed Morris. One stray cat in particular, which had wandered around our territory, had been injured and was very weak and hungry. We shared our food with him but kept our distance, as our people were worried that his injury might be infectious. They set up a humane trap and hoped to entice him with soft food - thinking that if they caught him, they could get him to the vet. As they prepared to put food in the trap, Alex was so curious that he went inside the trap and of course, SLAM! Yep, Alex looked pretty pathetic, but our people just told him he was a good kitty and let him out. They were never able to catch the injured stray and he eventually quit coming around. I still wonder what might have happened to him.

For the most part it was just fine and dandy having other cats in the neighborhood, as there were plenty of rodents and lizards to feed us all. However, as with most neighborhoods, there was one particular domestic house cat that seemed intent on being a nuisance. Maybe she just really liked me - after all, I am quite handsome. Or maybe she was jealous because our people were so much nicer than her people. I had heard from various neighborhood animals that her house was an unhappy and gloomy one. Regardless of the reason, she spent countless days watching my hunting and going out of her way to be catty. Jenny was a pure-bred Siamese - many of us just called her "Princess of the Valley". She would chase the mice into my hunting territory, and when I caught one, she would have a big hissy fit claiming it was her mouse and that I did not have permission to catch it! Being a house cat, she certainly didn't need to be a huntress, but she sure knew how to ruin things for me. The first time she set me up, I made the mistake of taking the mouse back to her and apologizing. Her reaction was to spit at me and hiss. With all of her bragging about being pure-bred, you would think that she would have been taught how to behave properly. I thought that I was much smarter the second time it happened. I ignored her ranting and raving and turned to head home with the mouse, when she ordered her dog, Gillum, to come get me! Boy was he ugly - old and grey, smelled and looked like he never bathed and wasn't much smarter than a rock. I wasn't sure how quick he was, so I dropped the mouse and scampered up the closest tree. I could hear Jenny cursing at him the whole way home - what a wimpy dog.

I had a deep-down feeling that it would someday end up in a catfight and later learned to trust those feelings, as I was right. I am relieved to say, that I dealt with her the way any feral cat would, and after that day, she ceased to upset my hunting territory. In fact, I think she avoids the area at all costs now.

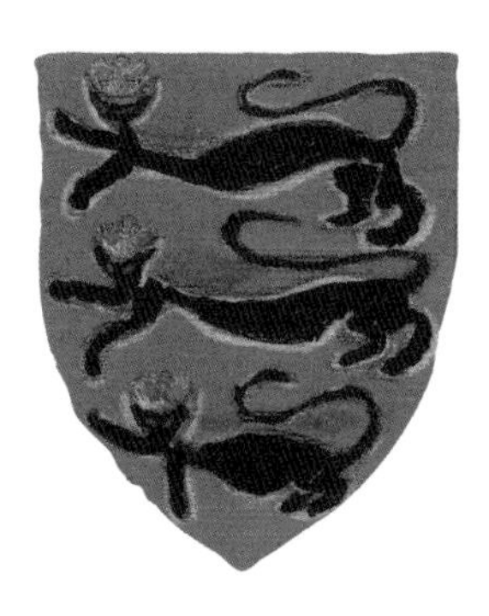

CHAPTER SIX

When I wasn't hunting or sleeping, I was honing my skills and entertaining myself - that's what cats do. Sometimes I would chase Morris just to annoy her and sometimes she would chase me. Alex and I would take turns being the prey, while the other one was the hunter, and we would signal each other with a flick of our tails. At times I felt as though we weren't just entertaining ourselves, but our people too. One day they came home with two new little animals - baby goats.

The dog took an instant dislike to the goats. He charged after them as our people unloaded them from the car. The goats were wearing collars held by lead ropes and very obviously felt threatened by the dog. Once the dog neared, each goat took off in the opposite direction, with one of our people still holding on. As the dog chased them around in circles, she became entangled in the ropes and her feet were flipped out from under her like a roped calf! Morris, Alex and I watched this from the safety of the deck. It took quite some time for everyone to get untangled - afterwards they were led to their stall.

Later, once the dog had been berated and all was quiet again, they told us, that they had been named, Wally and Buster. They were so small and cute and also extremely curious and talkative. Everything they smelled, they had to taste, and that included Morris, Alex and me! They did not simply smell and lick us they also pulled our hair. I don't believe that they meant to hurt us in any way, but we found it safer to sit on top of the barn rail and watch them explore.

Early the next morning, our people took Wally and Buster out to the pasture to graze - they were told that their job was to eat the grass, poison oak and wild berry bushes down to the nub. I thought it would be interesting to watch, so I followed them out to the pasture - Morris and Alex tagged along. They were chewing machines, and when they weren't eating or lying down for a rest, they were playing. Goats really enjoy their playtime, just like cats. They pretend to fight and butt heads, then run and kick up their heels. I joined in by sneaking up slowly behind them and once they noticed me, down went their heads and horns - the chase was on! We had loads of fun that day. Strange as it sounds, Wally could even climb a tree - sort of. With some momentum, he could actually go up on a low limb, but he couldn't get down. Many months later, he attempted to climb an oak tree for some leaves and found himself high-centered on a branch. Boy did he cry and cry for our people! By this time, he had gained some weight and was nearly one hundred pounds - one of our people really had her hands full getting him down.

Speaking of climbing adventures, one afternoon, Alex and I decided to have a contest to see who could climb to the uppermost part of the highest trees in the neighborhood. The two tallest stood mighty and daunting directly next to each other. To start, we cued one another with our tails and took off, racing across the grass! Further and further from the ground we got - we glanced over at each other to see who might be cowardly enough to stop first. I was so high I could see what seemed like the whole neighborhood. When I looked over at Alex one last time, in an instant, I lost my grip - sheer exhilaration turned into panic and dread. It was a long hard fall, hitting branches along the way, which luckily slowed my fall to the ground. I lay still for a few minutes to catch my breath - everything hurt. Alex scurried down and ran over to check on me - he asked if I was okay, but didn't touch me. Our people jumped down from the deck and talked softly to me while stroking my head gently. Once I snapped out of it, I inspected the damage - there were several deep scratches from the branches. I cleaned them up and took a good long nap.

By the next day, my entire right side was swollen and stiff, but I knew that I needed to get up and moving. Once outside, I stretched a bit and noticed our people - they opened the door on the deck and invited me in. I didn't feel well at all, but I was still leery about going into the house, having never been inside before. Of course all of those fears were quickly dashed when they brought out my favorite cheese. Then they shut the door behind me and WOW, those fears returned immediately - I was trapped! They put me into the old carrier that we were originally brought home in and told me that we were off to the vet. A scary experience for any cat, but for a feral cat, this was extremely unsettling.

After a short drive we arrived at the vet's office and sat down in the front room with all sorts of dogs and cats. Pretty soon a nurse took my carrier into a quiet room - my people came too and told me that it would all be okay. I was still skeptical. The doctor came in, gently examined me and told my people that I would need surgery due to the deep gashes caused by my fall. She said that they could come back to pick me up around dinnertime. As my people left, they made me a promise that everything would be okay and they would return for me soon. I was still shaking and very frightened, but was shortly calmed by the staff, who handled me tenderly. They let me know that I would be taking a short nap and that when I woke up I would feel much better. During that nap, I dreamt a lot and realized that I had come to trust people at last.

I woke up sort of dizzy, like my head was full of water with fish swimming around inside. I tried to raise my head but it was too heavy. Some time later, I realized that I was back in the cat carrier. Still sore, I checked myself out and found four tubes sticking out of my right side - and I had a large patch of missing hair. Oh, was I ever sleepy and thirsty! I must have dozed off again, because the next thing I knew, my people were there to get me. They were given all kinds of instructions from the doctor and then we proceeded to the car to return home. I assumed that I would go back to the barn but my people explained that the doctor insisted on me staying in the house for a couple of weeks. What I really wanted at that moment, was to go outside and have a good bath and find Alex and Morris and tell them EVERYTHING.

I hadn't even been inside for one day, but I really wanted to go outside! I kept telling my people over and over again, but they just stroked my head and talked softly, explaining that it was in my best interest to keep dirt out of the tubes. Yuck, those tubes - I wanted those out of me! Unfortunately, the vet's office put this stiff thing around my neck, which prevented me from reaching the tubes. Every time I got a chance, I repositioned myself in hopes of taking it off - but no luck. Each time I tried, I got closer and closer, but was always interrupted by one of my people. They picked me up and held me and gave me gentle rubs. I quickly learned exactly what that meant - time for a pill! I know that they were supposed to make me better, but they tasted yucky and I did not like having them shoved down my throat! This went on for days and days, and days. Even though I had to stay in the house, Alex and Morris were permitted supervised visits. Because I was too weak to play, I spent my time explaining to Alex why he needed to forget his nagging doubts about people in general. It took about a week, but he eventually let our people give him rubs and he in turn rubbed up against them. Morris preferred to watch from the door, and permitted our people just one rub at a time.

At last, a day that I had been looking forward to for a long time had finally come - I was almost completely healed and allowed to go back outside. I was FREE! The first thing I did was roll in the dirt and soak up the sunshine - I would never take these things for granted again. The area where I was still missing hair was quite tender and I found that it was smart to stay out of the berry bushes and the trees for a while longer. Alex, Morris and I played tag in the tall grass for hours and then retreated to the barn for a nap. After a couple of days, I realized that I missed cuddling with my people, so I divided my time between the house and the outside. If I stood on a potted plant situated by the front door window it would signal my people that I wanted to come in for a tummy rub. I guess you could say that I became a sort of a prince of the feral cats.

Being the observant cat that I am, I tend to see much more than simply what goes on in my own personal day - my mom used to jokingly call me "absorbent". I know that it is not always about me. I pay close attention to what goes on in the lives of my family members as well. I have come to the conclusion that there are lessons in all of life's adventures. We all have a story to tell, one that is unique to each and every one of us. I have learned a great deal by listening, and by watching the experiences of others as well. The beginning of my existence was not necessarily one that I would have chosen, but I recognize that through my misfortune and grief, I have come to appreciate all that I did have as a young kitten. My mother not only instilled skills, but morals in me - I didn't know I had them until I needed them. It could be that these skills are instinctual for all cats, but I am comforted to think that my mother did all she could in the short time she had with us. I have also observed and experienced myself that when we are wounded by actions or words, the pain of betrayal and loss causes us to look deep into our hearts, and in time, I have learned that we will heal. I also have found through various relationships, good and bad, that friends must earn my trust. These experiences have strengthened my trust in myself and taught me that I am strong and can get through anything. Family has also played a big role - both Alex and Morris have their quirks (as I'm sure I do) but I have gained much of my strength and perseverance from the bond of our unconditional family ties. I have also learned that it is indeed sometimes about the mouse, and that is okay. It's important to have a job to do each day and take pride in each task that it entails. Most importantly, it is crucial to have a safe haven, a home in which to take a nap, have a bath and be loved by your family, cats and people.

As I lay here on my favorite rock reflecting on all that I have been blessed with, I soak up the morning sun, my eyes fixed on the beauty of the valley. I can hear the playful clamor of my neighbor, Klaus. He is most probably bantering with the jackrabbits. The only cat I know that is actually fast enough to wrestle with one. The neighborhood is full of feral cats. We all strive, each day to keep our peoples' property free of rodents and lizards, which helps keep the rattlesnakes away, the livestock feed free of harmful droppings and the domestic house cats protected from wild animals. And in return for all that we do, our people provide us with a home, food, and all the scratches and tummy rubs that one feral cat can stand. What a purr-fectly princely existence.

~ The End.

A portion of the proceeds from the sale of this book will go to help fund AnimalSave's programs, including TNR*. AnimalSave, is a non-profit rescue organization in Grass Valley, CA. This is their message to the reader.

~

"Prince Jack and his siblings are very lucky feral kitties. They were rescued by caring people who helped find them a safe, forever home with loving guardians to look after them for rest of their lives.

Jack and his cohorts are fortunate because the community where he was found has a proactive group of volunteers and progressive animal welfare organizations to help kitties like him. Not many communities do.

The 3 most common ways ferals are dealt with are: 1- they are ignored, whereupon their numbers increase so much that they cannot be ignored, 2-they are killed by humans taking matters into their own hands either with a firearm or worse (like Jack's mom), 3- they are trapped and taken to a government-run animal control agency most of which do not have the resources, time, space, experience or mandate to spay, neuter, and find suitable homes. Most feral cats entering a government-run animal control agency are killed.

The fact is feral cats are a part of our urban and rural environments. Killing them has not decreased their numbers. In fact, many short-sighted communities have tried to eradicate ferals by killing them. Ultimately, however, other cats come in to take their places. This is called the vacuum effect. Unless the cats are spayed and neutered, the cycle continues.

The non-lethal process to decrease the number of feral cats in an area is called Trap-Neuter-Return. Once the cats are spayed or neutered and vaccinated, they are returned to their original homes. Because they are now altered, their population stabilizes and in the long term will decrease.

Many cities and towns in the U.S. and in Europe have been successful using this technique. Thus it is critical that ALL cats are spayed and neutered. This includes pet cats which are allowed outside, as well as strays that no one claims. One un-neutered male can impregnate many un-spayed females and they will travel long distances to find each other.

In our community we are lucky to have energetic volunteers willing to do the legwork and animal welfare agencies able to foot the vet bills to spay, neuter and vaccinate some of the "unwanted" ferals. These important resources exist only through generous donations of time, money and enthusiasm. Our community is doubly blessed by having a county-run animal control agency that currently understands and supports our goals. We hope that through our collaborative efforts and success at spaying/neutering and returning or placing feral cats, other government-run animal agencies and animal welfare organizations will follow suit. All of these groups cannot be taken for granted, however. As policies and individuals within organizations change, so can the flow of money and resources. We are working hard to show that this model of caring for ferals does not have to be a rarity, but instead can become the norm.

AnimalSave is one animal rescue group that helps feral cats as a part of its numerous animal welfare programs. Our Trap-Neuter-Return program has helped hundreds of feral cats get spayed, neutered and returned to their homes. In desperate cases, AnimalSave tries to re-home feral cats to safe barn-type situations where the humans are happy to have non-toxic rodent control supervising their property 24 hours a day.

We are grateful to be included in Suzanne Danforth's book about feral cats." ~ Carol Hyndman, board member of AnimalSave and owner of "The Country Cattery"

A portion of the proceeds from the sale of this book will go to help fund AnimalSave's programs, including TNR* (trap-neuter-release). AnimalSave, is a non-profit rescue organization in Grass Valley, CA. Its mission is to end the needless killing of adoptable/treatable companion animals and to ensure their humane treatment by creating a community pet adoption and education center; rescuing, fostering and placing homeless animals; encouraging spay/neuter; bringing animals and people together to enrich each others' lives; and promoting the concept that every companion animal deserves respect, as well as a loving home. For more information, contact www.animalsave.org or, Alley Cat Allies, which is a national non-profit group dedicated to helping feral cats. www.alleycat.org.

Credits:

Original artwork for this book created by Justin Danforth.

Photographs on title page, page 18 and page 19 by Bryan Danforth.

Author photo, photos on page 24 and 32 by Ryan Kitson.

This is a fictional book.
After all, when has a cat ever sat down and told his story?

Please send your comments and any special requests for braille or large print copies to the author at Jacktheferalprince@hotmail.com

The editor, Kathleen Wright, lives with her two cats, rescued from a no-kill facility in suburban Cincinnati, Ohio.

Gus

Roxie

Made in the USA
San Bernardino, CA
20 April 2014